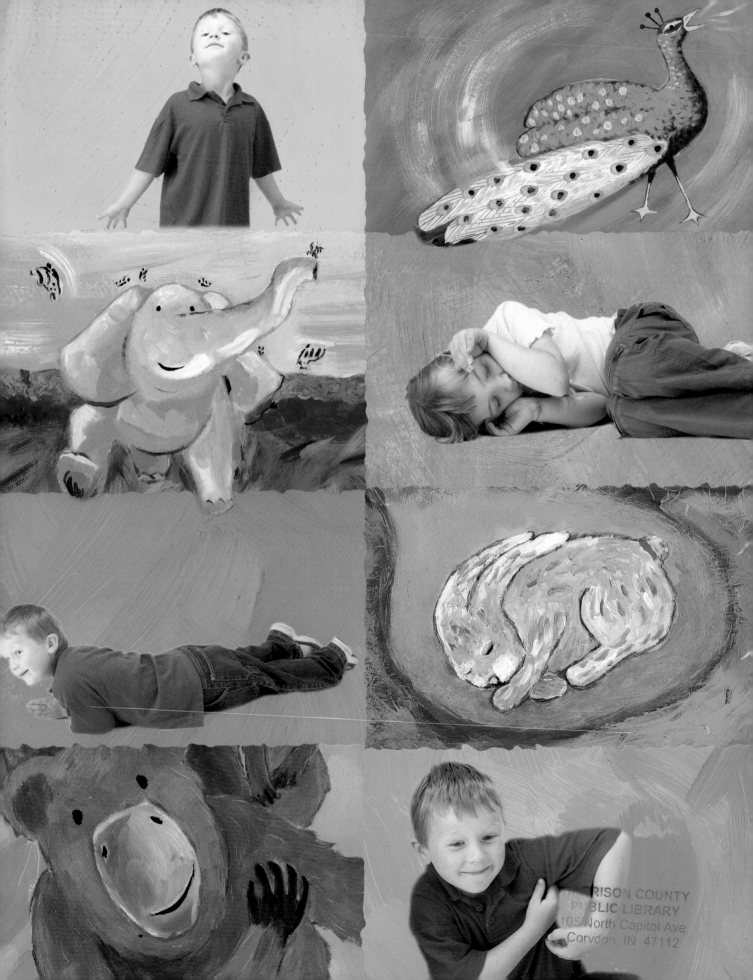

First edition for the United States, its territories and dependencies, Canada,
and the Philippines published in 2003 by Barron's Educational Series, Inc.

First published in 2003 by Transworld Publishers,
a division of The Random House Group Ltd

Designed by Ian Butterworth

All inquiries should be addressed to:
Barron's Educational Series, Inc.
250 Wireless Boulevard
Hauppauge, New York 11788
http://www.barronseduc.com

International Standard Book No. 0-7641-2586-9

Library of Congress Catalog Card No. 2003100773

Printed in Hong Kong
9 8 7 6 5 4 3 2 1

Can You Move Like an Elephant?

Judy Hindley Illustrated by **Manya Stojic**

BARRON'S

Can you do what an
elephant does?

Deep in the jungle,
the elephants go —
slow, slow, to and fro,
swinging their trunks
from side to side.

Boom!
Boom!

the elephants go.

Can you go
like that?

Can you go like a
slithery snake?
A slithery snake
curls up so small
and wiggles
and wiggles
and writhes . . .
twisting
her body from
side to side.

Can you leap
out of reach like
a monkey does?
Can you go swinging
from branch to
branch,
and huddle in
snuggly bunches
together
to cuddle and
chatter and
snatch?

**Can you do
a monkey
scratch?**

Can you hold up
your head like a
peacock does?
Can you walk so proud?
Can you cry so loud?

Awk! Awk!
swishing your
tail from side
to side.

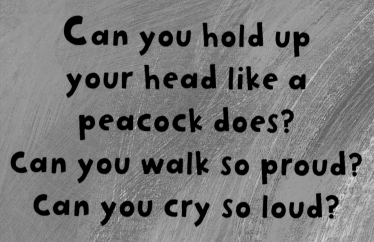

Can you do that?

Can you go as slow as a silvery snail, reaching and searching with delicate horns, stretching his stone-colored, moon-colored body, long and skinny and slim?

Can you stretch out like him?

And then can you
QUIVER
as quick as a flame
like a butterfly
wavering,
flower to flower,
silently flickering
big, bright
wings?

Can you
do that?

Can you go
like a tiger goes,
silently stalking
her prey —
slinking
ever so
slowly and
low to the
ground . . .
till she crouches
and
springs
in a glorious bound.

Can you
do that?

And can you go
like a startled
deer,
when she
picks up her head
and
FREEZES
with
fear —
and then goes
springing
away?

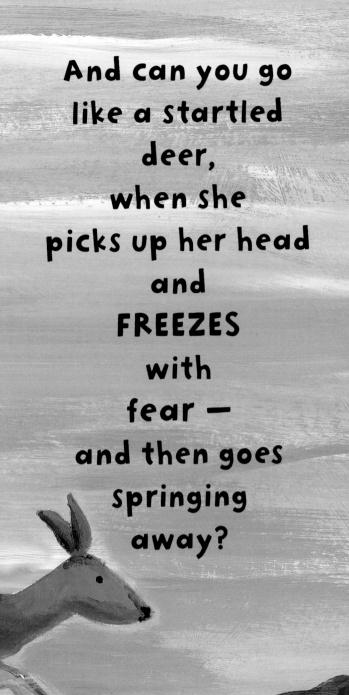

Can you
do that?

Can you wheel and whirl like a terrified herd, when the tiger is following faster and faster;

turn on your hooves all together like dancers, and slip like the wind from her pursuit?

Can you shift and turn like that?

Can you lift
your wings like
huge flamingos,
brushing
their feathers
like fingers
together,
in ripples of
color that cover
the sun,
circling the sky
until danger is
gone?

Can you ripple
and swing
like that?

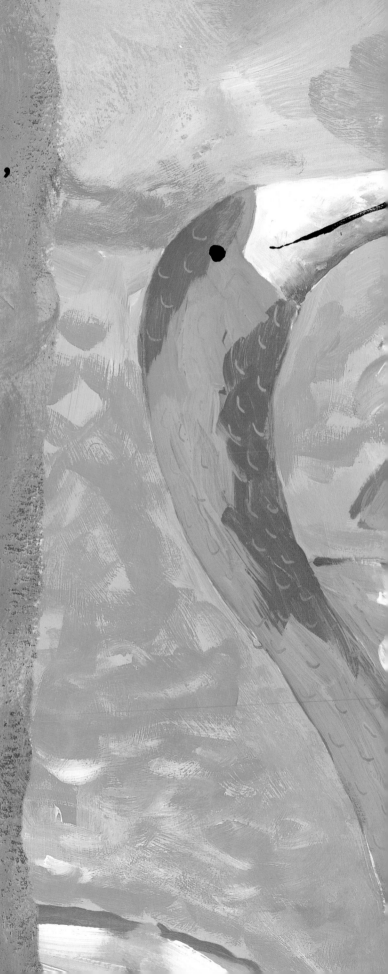

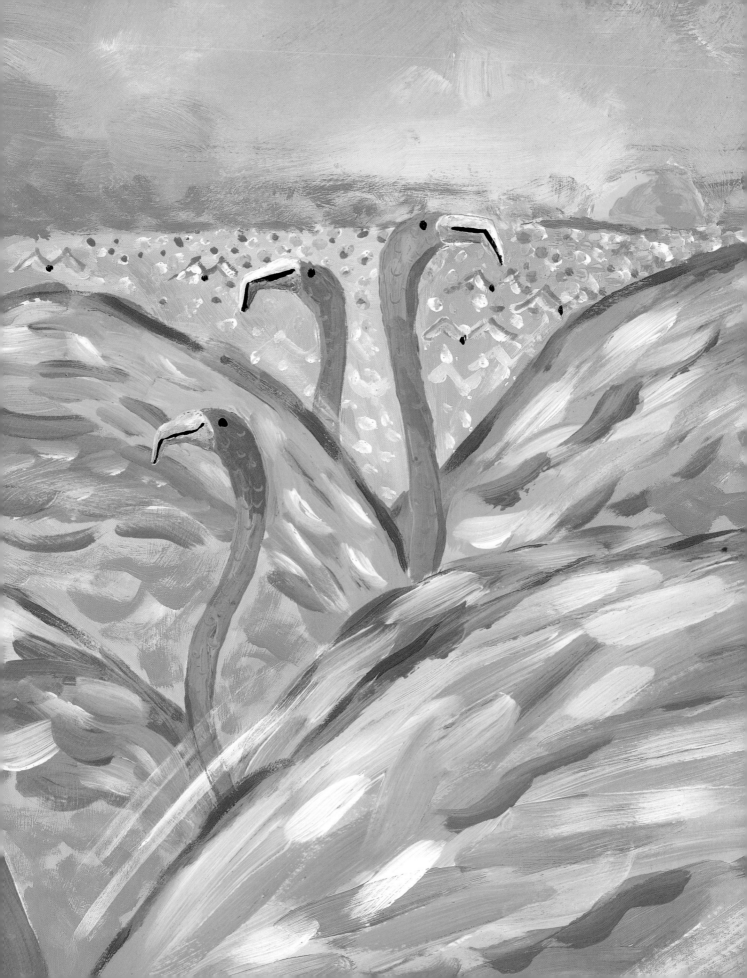

And can you go like a small, gray rabbit, who dives in his burrow, and sinks to his rest, settling soft as a small, gray cloud, with his head bending gently to his chest?

Can you be as quiet and peaceful as that?

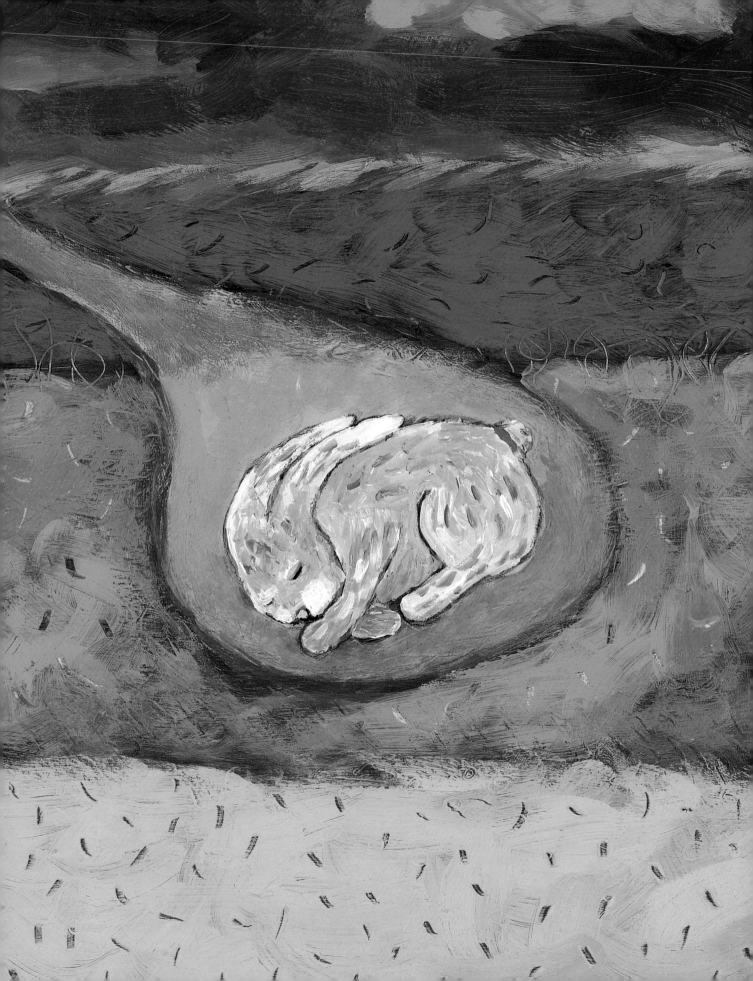

Can you sleep so sweet
at the end of the
day?

Can you sleep
like that?

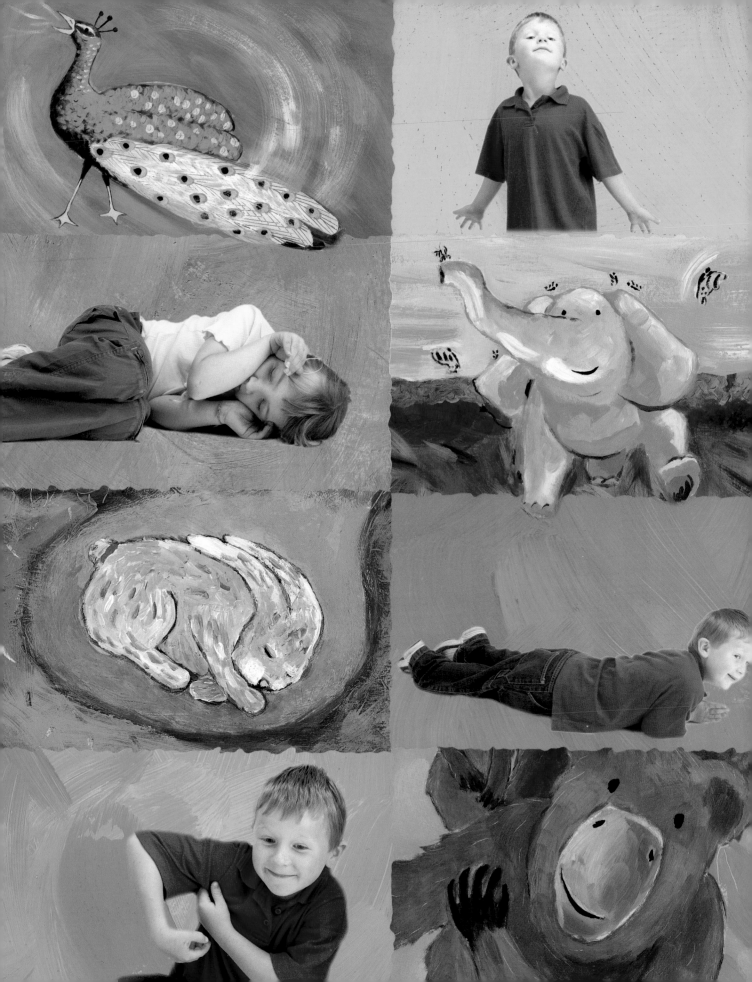